# Barnyard Chase!

p

Mother Hen sat on her nest and shook out her soft, fluffy feathers. She had an egg to keep warm. She had been sitting there for hours.

"I'm hungry," thought Mother Hen. But there was no grain nearby for her to peck.

Suddenly, Mother Hen saw a patch of sunlight by the barn door. She had an idea. She rolled her egg carefully over into the sun and packed some hay around it.

"That will keep you warm," she said to her egg. "I won't be long." And off she went to find some grain.

Horse came trotting
up to the barn. He was
hungry, too. He saw the
hay that Mother Hen had
piled by the barn door.

"Yummy!" he neighed, as he pushed his smooth, velvety muzzle into the hay. **Bump!** Horse's nose nudged the egg.

The egg rocked, and then it rolled. It rolled across the yard.

"Oh, no!" neighed Horse. "Catch that egg before it cracks!" And he trotted after the egg as it tumbled toward a pile of apples under the apple tree.

Pig was snuffling around under the apple tree.
He was hungry, too.

"Yummy!" he grunted, as he pushed his
squashy, squidgy snout into the pile of apples.

**Bump!** Pig's nose knocked against the egg.

The egg rocked, and then it rolled. It rolled along the lane.

"Oh, no!" squealed Pig. "Catch that egg before it cracks!" And he scampered after the egg as it tumbled into the grassy meadow.

Sheep was munching the tufty grass in the meadow. She was hungry, too.

"Yummy!" she baaa-ed, as she poked her frizzy, fleecy face into the grass.

**Bump!** She banged her nose against the egg. The egg rocked, and then it rolled. It rolled down the hill.

"Oh, no!" bleated Sheep. "Catch that egg before it cracks!" And she skipped after the egg as it tumbled down the hill.

At the bottom of the hill, Cow was lying
down, taking a rest after lunch. Bump!
The egg bounced against Cow's soft, silky nose.
"Ouch!" mooed Cow. "What was that?"
And she stared at the egg.

Horse, Pig, and Sheep came running down the hill.

"Catch that egg before it cracks!" they called.

"I have caught it," replied Cow.
Just then, there was a loud CRACK!
"My egg!" clucked Hen, as she came
flapping down the hill.

They all looked at the cracked egg. "Oh, no!" neighed Horse. CRACK! The crack got bigger.

"I didn't break it!" grunted Pig. CRACK! The crack got even bigger.

"I didn't break it, either!" bleated Sheep. CRACK! The crack got bigger still.

"Well, it wasn't me!" mooed Cow.

"Someone must have cracked it!" clucked Hen.